Little Red
and the
Very Hungry
LION

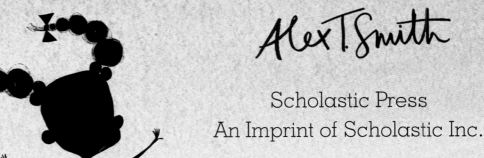

Alex T. Smith

Scholastic Press
An Imprint of Scholastic Inc.

This is Little Red.
Today she is going to be gobbled up by a lion.

This is the Lion!
(Well, that's what he thinks is going to happen anyway.)

One hot morning, Auntie Rosie woke up covered in **spots**.

There was only one thing for them: spot medicine.

RING! RING! RING! RING! RING!

"Oh, dear! Oh, dear!" said Little Red when she heard the news. "I'll come right away!"

THE
LL-YOU-NEED
GENERAL STORE

SNIP-SNIP BARBER

BEST CUTS IN TOWN!

FRUIT &
VEGGIES

SPOT
MEDICINE

FRESH
DOUGHNUTS

So she put some
spot medicine
in her basket
and waved
good-bye to
her daddy.

over
the sleepy
crocodiles,

It was a long way to
Auntie Rosie's house.

Little Red walked under
the **giraffes,**

and past
the chattering
monkeys.

She crept around the
termite mounds
and under the
leaping gazelles.

Then she caught a ride
on an elephant,

wiggled her
way around the
hippos and **warthogs,**

and waved hello
to the **meerkats.**

Then she sat down in the shade of a shady tree.

And that's when the Lion arrived —

the Very
Hungry Lion.

"Oh, hello," purred the Lion.
"Where are you going?"

"To visit my auntie who is
covered in spots," said Little Red.

In the time it took for his tummy
to rumble, the Very Hungry Lion
had cooked up a

very
naughty
plan.

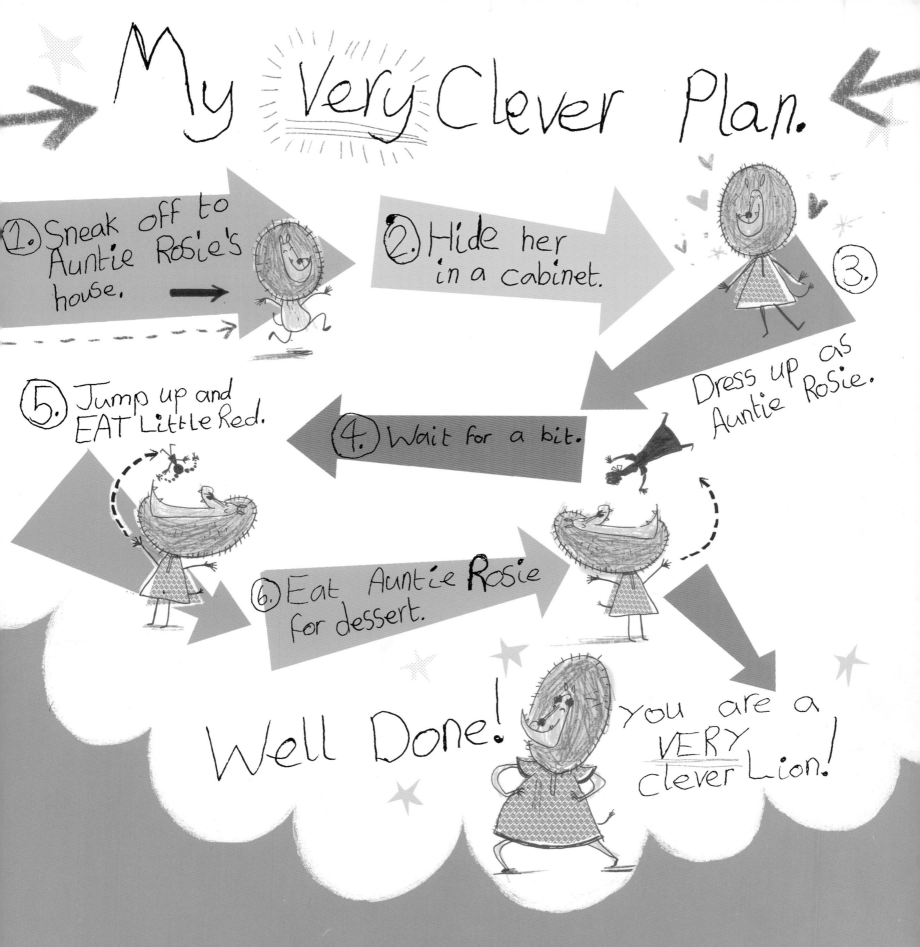

My Very Clever Plan.

1. Sneak off to Auntie Rosie's house.

2. Hide her in a cabinet.

3. Dress up as Auntie Rosie.

4. Wait for a bit.

5. Jump up and EAT Little Red.

6. Eat Auntie Rosie for dessert.

Well Done! You are a VERY clever Lion!

And he rushed off to put his plan into action.

When he arrived, the Very Hungry Lion stuffed Auntie Rosie in a cabinet and locked the door.

Then he squeeeeezed himself into one of her nightgowns and covered himself all over in spots.

Of course, when Little Red arrived, she realized right away it wasn't Auntie Rosie sitting in the bed.

She quickly looked around and spotted her auntie peeking through a gap in the cabinet.

Then Little Red decided that she was going to teach the naughty Lion a lesson!

"Oh, Auntie!" cried Little Red.
"What tangled **hair** you have!"

And before the Very Hungry Lion
could even lick his lips, Little Red

had **brushed**

and **combed**

and
twisted
and
braided
until the Lion had
a
lovely
new look.

This had **not** been part of the Lion's plan.

So . . .

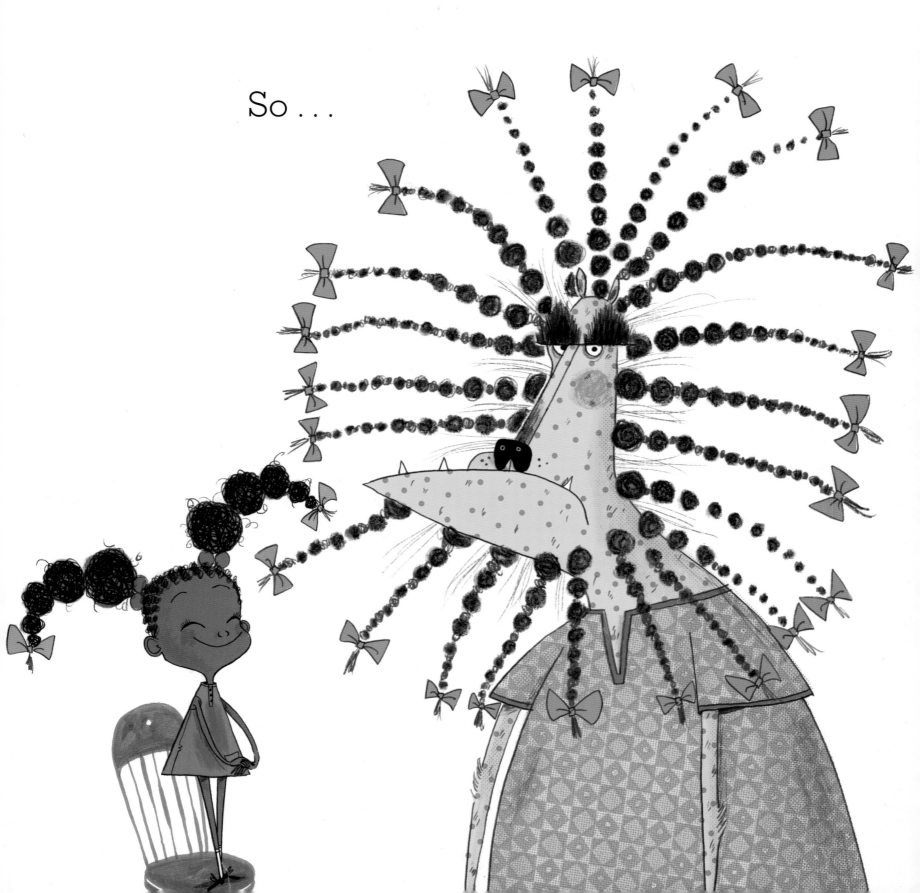

He opened his mouth wide.

"Disgusting!"

shouted Little Red.

"What gigantic, grimy teeth you have, Auntie!"

And Little Red made
the Very Hungry Lion
brush,
brush,
brush
his teeth until
they sparkled.

"Oh, Auntie!" sighed Little Red.
"What an old **nightgown** you are wearing!"

And before the Very Hungry Lion
knew it, Little Red had
found a **much**
prettier dress for him
to wear.

This had **not** been part of
the Lion's plan, either.

TOP!

yelled the Lion.

"I am a Very Hungry Lion,

and my tummy is grumbling!"

The Very Hungry Lion let Auntie Rosie out of the cabinet and said SORRY ever so politely.

Little Red gave Auntie Rosie the spot medicine, which worked immediately.

Little Red pointed her finger.

"Well, trying to eat children and aunties is VERY naughty. If you were hungry, all you had to do was ask for some food."

Then the three of them
gobbled up a whole basket
of **doughnuts** together.

(The Lion had **five**.)

Soon it was beginning
to get dark, so the Lion
walked all the way
back home with Little Red
on his **very** best behavior.
He promised to

**never, ever,
ever**

try to eat another auntie
or any children.

But he **might** be tempted to **eat Daddy!**

NO!
Bad Kitty!

THE END